Engineer Arielle and the Israel Independence Day Surprise

D1160099

Mid-pirouette, Arielle heard her brother Ezra laugh.
"You're certainly happy today!"
"Of course I am!" said Arielle. "It's Israel's birthday!
Yom Ha'Atzma'ut!"

"It's too bad that we both have to work today while everybody else has a holiday," said Ezra. "We won't even get to see each other."

"Not true," Arielle reminded him. "I'll see you, even if you don't see me. Everybody in Israel will see you today!"

"I suppose you're right," chuckled Ezra.

Arielle looked at her watch. "Oops, I've got to go."

Arielle jumped onto her scooter, tucking her poster behind her seat. She zoomed off, weaving through Jerusalem's traffic.

Beep, beep! She passed the old train station. Trains no longer stopped at the old station. Now, cafes filled the space.

Arielle thought of her great-great-grandfather, Engineer Ari, who drove the first train from Tel Aviv to Jerusalem into that very station over 100 years ago. Arielle was named after him. "Great-Great-Grandpa Ari," whispered Arielle. "I'm a train engineer, just like you!"

Arielle rode her scooter up a hill and down into a valley. She passed falafel stands, vegetable markets, and playgrounds.

Beep, beep, zoom, zoom!

In her conductor's seat, Arielle sat in front of
her controls—computer screens, knobs, and levers.
Lickety split, she started the train and pulled out
of the station, right on time.

The train hummed toward its first stop. The doors opened with a buzz. Passengers piled into the train. "**Yom Ha'Atzma'ut sameach!**" called Arielle cheerfully. "**Happy Independence Day!**"

The train hummed through Jerusalem, picking up passengers and dropping them off. **RinG, rinG.** *Buzz, buzz.* Doors opened. Doors closed. *Hum, hum.* The train stopped at the Old City. A computerized voice announced, "Damascus Gate."

Arielle saw her friend Sarah getting off the train. "**Yom Ha'Atzma'ut sameach**, Sarah! Where are you headed?"

"I'm going to the Kotel," said Sarah. "Every Independence Day, I go to the Western Wall to put a note into the Wall praying for peace in Israel. How will you celebrate today, Arielle?"

"I'm going to celebrate with my brother. We'll all celebrate with him!"

"What do you mean?" asked Sarah.

But before Arielle could answer, Sarah was swept up in the crowd leaving the train, and waving good-bye.

Buzz, buzz. The doors closed. *Hum, hum.* The train started up a small hill. Arielle stopped the train at a large market. The computerized voice announced, "Machane Yehuda." Arielle saw her neighbor Eitan.

"Ah, Arielle," said Eitan. "I thought my wife had bought food for our Yom Ha'Atzma'ut barbecue. But *she* thought that *I* bought it. So, here I am at the *shuk*, the market. Are you going to a picnic or barbecue after work to celebrate the holiday?"

"I'll see my brother Ezra later," said Arielle. "And I'll celebrate with him. We'll all celebrate with him!"

"All Israel celebrates together, doesn't it?" said Eitan. "One *mishpachah*, one family."

Buzz, buzz. The doors closed. *Hum, hum.* The train continued on. Arielle pulled into the train stop at the central bus station. From there, travelers could go anywhere in Israel.

Arielle saw two of her friends getting off the train with backpacks.

"Jesse! Benny! Where are you headed?"

"Tel Aviv," said Benny.

"I'm going to visit Independence Hall, where David Ben-Gurion declared Israel a country in 1948," said Jesse.

"I just want to go to the beach," laughed Benny. "Come with us, Arielle."

"I can't," laughed Arielle. "I have a train to drive. Besides, I'll see my brother later and celebrate with him. We'll all celebrate with him!"

"Bring your brother to Tel Aviv!" called Benny.

"He's already going to Tel Aviv," laughed Arielle. "And to Haifa, Tiberias, Beersheva, and Eilat."

Buzz, buzz. The doors closed. *Hum, hum.* The train continued on, over a magnificent bridge built to look like King David's harp.

Arielle held her breath as Ezra's plane roared through the sky.

Then Ezra dipped low toward the train bridge.
He waved from the cockpit.

Arielle and the passengers cheered.
"Yom Ha'Atzma'ut sameach!"

Happy Independence Day, Israel!

Author's Note

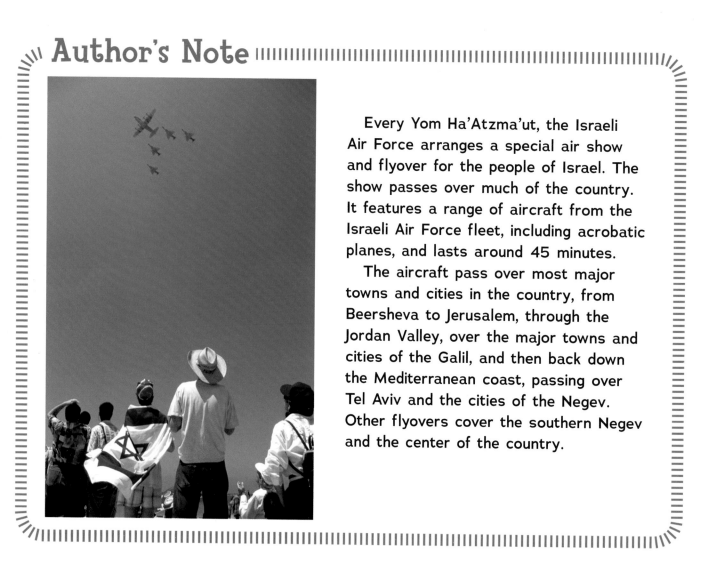

Every Yom Ha'Atzma'ut, the Israeli Air Force arranges a special air show and flyover for the people of Israel. The show passes over much of the country. It features a range of aircraft from the Israeli Air Force fleet, including acrobatic planes, and lasts around 45 minutes.

The aircraft pass over most major towns and cities in the country, from Beersheva to Jerusalem, through the Jordan Valley, over the major towns and cities of the Galil, and then back down the Mediterranean coast, passing over Tel Aviv and the cities of the Negev. Other flyovers cover the southern Negev and the center of the country.